James Townley

High Life Below Stairs

A Farce of two Acts

James Townley

High Life Below Stairs
A Farce of two Acts

ISBN/EAN: 9783743418851

Manufactured in Europe, USA, Canada, Australia, Japa

Cover: Foto ©Andreas Hilbeck / pixelio.de

Manufactured and distributed by brebook publishing software
(www.brebook.com)

James Townley

High Life Below Stairs

HIGH LIFE

BELOW STAIRS.

A

FARCE

OF

TWO ACTS.

As it is performed at the

Theatre-Royal in Drury-Lane.

O imitatores, Servum pecus ! HOR.

The SEVENTH EDITION.

LONDON:

'rinted for J. NEWBERY, at the Bible and Sun in
St. Paul's Church-Yard ; R. BAILYE, at Litchfield ;
J. LEAKE and W. FREDERICK, at Bath ; B. COLLINS,
at Salisbury ; and S. STABLER, at York.

MDCCLXIII.
[Price One Shilling.]

Dramatis Perſonæ.

Lovel, *a young* Weſt-Indian *of Fortune,*		Mr. Obrien.
Freeman, *his Friend,*		Mr. Packer.
Philip,		Mr. Yates.
Tom,		Mr. Mozn.
Coachman,		Mr. Clough.
Kingston, *a Black,*	*Servants to* Lovel.	Mr. Moody.
Kitty,		Mrs. Clive.
Cook,		Mrs. Bradshaw.
Cloe, a *Black,*		Mrs. Smith.
Duke's Ser-vant,		Mr. Palmer.
Sir Harry's Servant,		Mr. King.
Lady Bab's Maid,	*Viſitors.*	Miſs Hippisley.
Lady Char-lqtte's Mai.		Mrs. Bennet.
Robert, *Servant to* Freeman,		Mr. Acman.
Fidler,		Mr. Atkins.

SCENE, *London.*

✛✛✛ ✛✛✛✛✛✛✛✛✛✛✛✛✛✛✛✛✛✛✛✛✛✛✛✛✛

ADVERTISEMENT.

IT was a real Deſire to do good, amongſt a very large and uſeful Body of People, that gave Riſe to this little Piece. The Author thought the Stage, where the Bad might be diſgrac'd, and the Good rewarded, the moſt ready and effectual Me-thod for this Purpoſe: And, as he never wrote before in the Dramatic Way, and was unwilling to be known, he was happy in recommending the Performance, by the Aſſiſtance of a Friend, to the Care and Judgment of Mr. Garrick.

Nov. 5, 1759.

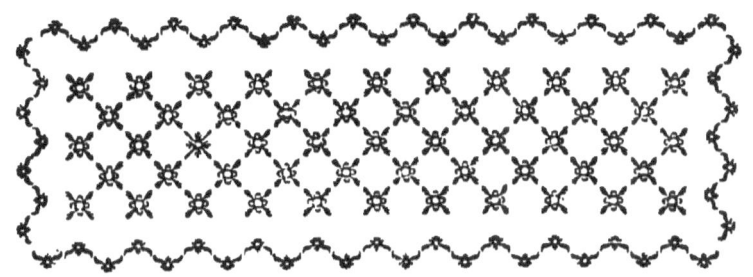

HIGH LIFE
BELOW STAIRS.

ok°ock°ok° *°ok°ok° ok°ok°ok° ok°ok°ok°ok°ok° ok°ok°ok°ok°ok° ok°ok°ok°ok°

A C T I.

SCENE, *An Apartment in* Freeman's *Houfe.*

FREEMAN *and* LOVEL, *entering.*

FREEMAN.

Country Boy! ha, ha, ha. How long has this Scheme been in your Head?

LOVEL.

Some Time—I am now convinc'd of what you have often been hinting to me, that I am confoundedly cheated by my Servants.

FREEMAN.

Oh! are you fatisfied at laft, Mr. *Lovel?* I always told you, that there is not a worfe Set of Servants in the Parifh of St. *James*'s, than in your Kitchen.

LOVEL.

'Tis with fome Difficulty I believe it now, Mr. *Freeman*; tho', I muft own, my Expences often

A 2 make

make me ftare — *Philip*, I am fure, is an honeft Fellow ; and I will fwear for my Blacks — If there is a Rogue among my Folks, it is that furly Dog *Tom*.

F R E E M A N.

You are miftaken in every one. *Philip* is an hypocritical Rafcal : *Tom* has a good deal of furly Honefty about him : and for your Blacks, they are as bad as your Whites.

L O V E L.

Prithee, *Freeman*, how came you to be fo well acquainted with my People ? None of the Wenches are handfome enough to move the Affections of a middle-aged Gentleman as you are. Ha, ha, ha.

F R E E M A N.

You are a young Man, Mr. *Lovel*, and take a Pride in a Number of idle, unneceffary Servants, who are the Plague and Reproach of this Kingdom.

L O V E L.

Charles, you are an old-fafhion'd Fellow. Servants a Plague and Reproach ! ha, ha, ha. I would have forty more, if my Houfe would hold them. Why, Man, in *Jamaica*, before I was ten Years old, I had a hundred Blacks kiffing my Feet every Day.

F R E E M A N.

You Gentry of the Weftern Ifles are high-mettled Ones, and love Pomp and Parade — I have feen it delight your Soul, when the People in the Street have ftared at your Equipage ; efpecially if they whifper'd loud enough to be heard, " That is " 'Squire *Lovel*, the great *Weft-India*." Ha, ha, ha.

L O V E L.

I fhould be very forry if we were as fplenetic as you Northern Iflanders, who are devoured with Melancholy and Fog. Ha, ha, ha! No, Sir, we

are

are Children of the Sun, and are born to diffuse the bounteous Favour which our noble Parent is pleased to bestow on us.

FREEMAN.

I wish you had more of your noble Parent's Regularity, and less of his Fire. As it is, you consume so fast, that not one in twenty of you live to be fifty Years old.

LOVEL.

But in that fifty we live two hundred, my Dear; mark that. — But to Business — I am resolv'd upon my Frolick — I will know whether my Servants are Rogues or not. If they are, I'll bastinado the Rascals; if not, I think I ought to pay for my Impertinence. — Pray tell me; is not your *Robert* acquainted with my People? Perhaps he may give a little light into the Thing.

FREEMAN.

To tell you the Truth, Mr. *Lovel*, your Servants are so abandoned, that I have forbid him your House — However, if you have a Mind to ask him any Question, he shall be forthcoming.

LOVEL.

Let us have him.

FREEMAN.

You shall; but it is an hundred to one if you get any thing out of him; for, though he is a very honest Fellow, yet he is so much of a Servant, that he'll never tell any thing to the Disadvantage of another — Who waits? [*Enter Servant.*] Send *Robert* to me — [*Exit Servant.*] And what was it determin'd you upon this Project at last?

LOVEL.

This Letter. It is an anonymous one, and so ought not to be regarded; but it has something honest in it, and put me upon satisfying my Curiosity. — Read it.   [*Gives the Letter.*

FREEMAN.

FREEMAN.

I fhould know fomething of this Hand—[*Reads.*

" *To* Peregrine Lovel, *Efq*;

" Pleafe your Honour,

" I take the Liberty to acquaint your Honour,
" that you are fadly cheated by your Servants.—
" Your Honour will find it as I fay.——I am not
" willing to be known, whereof, if I am, it may
" bring one into Trouble.

" So no more, from your Honour's
" Servant to command."

—Odd and honeft! Well—and now what are the
Steps you intend to take? —— [*Returns the Letter.*

LOVEL.

I fhall immediately apply to my Friend the Ma-
nager for a Difguife—Under the Form of a gawky
Country Boy, I will be an Eye-witnefs of my
Servants Behaviour —— you muft affift me, Mr.
Freeman.

FREEMAN.

As how? Mr. *Lovel.*

LOVEL.

My Plan is this —— I gave it out, that I was
going to my Borough in *Devonfhire*, and Yefterday
fet out with a Servant in great Form, and lay at
Bafingftoke.——

FREEMAN.

Well?

LOVEL.

I order'd the Fellow to make the beft of his Way
down into the Country, and told him that I would
follow him; inftead of that, I turn'd back, and am
juft come to Town: *Ecce Signum!*——[*Points to
his boots.*

FREEMAN.

It is now One o'Clock.

LOVEL.

This very Afternoon I fhall pay my People a
Vifit.

FREEMAN.

FREEMAN.

How will you get in?

LOVEL.

When I am properly habited, you ſhall get me introduc'd to *Philip* as one of your Tenants Sons, who wants to be made a good Servant of.

FREEMAN.

They will certainly diſcover you.

LOVEL.

Never fear; I'll be ſo countrify'd, that you ſhall not know me.—As they are thoroughly perſuaded I am many Miles off, they'll be more eaſily impoſed on. Ten to one but they begin to celebrate my Departure with a drinking Bout, if they are what you deſcribe them.————

FREEMAN.

Shall you be able to play your Part?

LOVEL.

I am ſurpriz'd, Mr. *Freeman*, that you, who have known me from my Infancy, ſhould not remember my Abilities in that Way. But you old Fellows have ſhort Memories.

FREEMAN.

What ſhould I remember?

LOVEL.

How I play'd *Daniel* in the *Conſcious Lovers* at School, and afterwards arriv'd at the diſtinguiſh'd Character of the mighty Mr. *Scrub*.————

[*Mimicking.*

FREEMAN.

Ha, ha, ha! That is very well.—Enough.——— Here is *Robert*.

Enter Robert.

Your Honour order'd me to wait on you.

FREEMAN.

I did, *Robert*——*Robert*——

ROBERT.

ROBERT.

Sir————

FREEMAN.

Come here—You know, *Robert*, I have a good Opinion of your Integrity.——

ROBERT.

I have always endeavour'd that your Honour fhould.

FREEMAN.

Pray, have not you fome Acquaintance among Mr. *Lovel*'s People?

ROBERT.

A little, pleafe your Honour.

FREEMAN.

How do they behave? — We have nobody but Friends——You may fpeak out.

LOVEL.

Ay, *Robert*, fpeak out.

ROBERT.

I hope your Honours will not infift on my faying any thing in an Affair of this Kind.

LOVEL.

Oh, but we do infift—If you know any thing.—

ROBERT.

Sir, I am but a Servant myfelf, and it would not become me to fpeak ill of a Brother Servant.

FREEMAN.

Pfha! This is falfe Honefty—fpeak out.

ROBERT.

Don't oblige me, good Sir.——Confider, Sir, a Servant's Bread depends upon his *Carackter*.

LOVEL.

But if a Servant ufes me ill——

ROBERT.

Alas! Sir, what is one Man's Poifon is another Man's Meat.

FREEMAN.

FREEMAN.

You see how they trim for one another.

ROBERT.

Service, Sir, is no Inheritance.—A Servant that is not approv'd in one Place, may give Satisfaction in another. Every Body muſt live, your Honour.

LOVEL.

Robert, I like your Heartineſs, as well as your Caution; but in my Caſe, it is neceſſary that I ſhould know the Truth.

ROBERT.

The Truth, ſir, is not to be ſpoken at all Times; it may bring one into Trouble, whereof if——

FREEMAN. *(Muſing.)*

" Whereof if " — Pray, Mr. *Lovel*, let me ſee that Letter again [Lovel *gives the Letter.*]—Aye— It muſt be ſo—*Robert ?*

ROBERT.

Sir.

FREEMAN.

Do you know any thing of this Letter?

ROBERT.

Letter, your Honour?

FREEMAN.

Yes, Letter?

ROBERT.

I have ſeen the Hand before.

LOVEL.

He bluſhes !

FREEMAN.

I aſk you, If you were concern'd in writing this Letter ?—You never told me a Lye yet, and I expect the Truth from you now.

ROBERT.

Pray your Honour, don't aſk me.

FREEMAN.

Did you write it ?—Anſwer me?——

B   ROBERT.

ROBERT.

I cannot deny it.   [*Bowing.*

LOVEL.

What induc'd you to it?

ROBERT.

I will tell Truth. — I have feen fuch Wafte and
Extravagance, and Riot and Drunkenefs, in your
Kitchen, Sir, that, as my mafter's Friend, I could
not help difcovering it to you.

LOVEL.

Go on.

ROBERT.

I am forry to fay it to your Honour; but your
Honour is not only impofed on, but laught at by
all your Servants; efpecially by *Philip*, who is a
——very bad Man.

LOVEL.

Philip? An ungrateful Dog! — Well?

ROBERT.

I could not prefume to fpeak to your Honour;
and therefore, I refolv'd, though but a poor Scribe,
to write your Honour a Letter.

LOVEL.

Robert, I am greatly indebted to you.—Here—
                                   [*Offers Money.*

ROBERT.

On any other Account than this, I fhould be
proud to receive your Honour's Bounty; but now
I beg to be excus'd——   [*Refufes the Money.*

LOVEL.

Thou haft a noble Heart, *Robert*, and I'll not
forget you.—*Freeman*, he muft be in the Secret—
Wait your Mafter's Orders.——

ROBERT.

I will, your Honour.   [*Exit.*

FREEMAN.

Well, Sir, are you convinc'd now?

LOVEL.

LOVEL.

· Convinc'd ? Yes; and I'll be among the Scoundrels before Night—You or *Robert* muſt contrive ſome Way or other to get me introduc'd to *Philip*, as one of your Cottager's Boys out of *Eſſex*.

FREEMAN.

Ha, ha, ha! you'll make a fine Figure.

LOVEL.

They ſhall make a fine Figure. —— It muſt be done this Afternoon; walk with me acroſs the *Park*, and I'll tell you the Whole.—My Name ſhall be *Jemmy*——And I am come to be a Gentleman's Servant—and will do my beſt, and hope to get a good *Carackter*. [*Mimicking.*

FREEMAN.

But what will you do if you find them Raſcals?

LOVEL.

Diſcover myſelf, and blow them all to the Devil. ——Come along——

FREEMAN.

Ha, ha, ha! ——Bravo——*Jemmy*——Bravo, ha, ha! [*Exeunt.*

SCENE, *The Park,*

DUKE's Servant.

What Wretches are ordinary Servants that go on in the ſame vulgar Track ev'ry Day! Eating, working, and ſleeping!——But we, who have the Honour to ſerve the Nobility, are of another Species. We are above the common Forms, have Servants to wait upon us, and are as lazy and luxurious as our Maſters.——Ha!——My dear Sir *Harry*.——

(Enter Sir HARRY's *Servant.)*

——How have you done theſe thouſand Years?

Sir

Sir H A R R Y.

My Lord Duke!—your Grace's moſt obedient Servant.

D U K E.

Well, Baronet, and where have you been?

Sir H A R R Y.

At *Newmarket*, my Lord—We have had dev'liſh fine Sport.

D U K E.

And a good Appearance, I hear.—Pox take it, I ſhould have been there; but our old Duchefs died, and we were oblig'd to keep Houſe, for the Decency of the Thing.

Sir H A R R Y.

I pick'd up fifteen Pieces.

D U K E.

Pſha! a Trifle!

Sir H A R R Y.

The Viſcount's People have been bloodily taken in this Meeting.

D U K E.

Credit me, Baronet, they know nothing of the Turf.

Sir H A R R Y.

I aſſure you, my Lord, they loſt every Match; for *Crab* was beat hollow, *Careleſs* threw his Rider, and Miſs *Slammerkin* had the Diſtemper.

D U K E.

Ha, ha, ha! I'm glad on't.——Taſte this Snuff, Sir *Harry*.   [*Offers his Box.*

Sir H A R R Y.

'Tis good Rapee.

D U K E.

Right *Straſburgh*, I aſſure you, and of my own importing.

Sir H A R R Y.

Aye!

D U K E.

DUKE.

The City People adulterate it fo confoundedly, that I always import my own Snuff.—I wifh my Lord would do the fame; but he is fo indolent.—When did you fee the Girls? I faw Lady *Bab* this Morning; but, 'fore Gad, whether it be Love or Reading, fhe look'd as Pale as a Penitent.

Sir HARRY.

I have juft had this Card from *Lovel*'s People—(*Reads.*) " *Philip* and Mrs. *Kitty* prefent their " Compliments to Sir *Harry*, and defire the Ho-" nour of his Company this Evening, to be of a " fmart Party, and to eat a Bit of Supper."

DUKE.

I have the fame Invitation — Their Mafter, it feems, is gone to his Borough.

Sir HARRY.

You'll be with us, my Lord? —— *Philip*'s a Blood.————

DUKE.

A Buck of the firft Head. I'll tell you a Secret, he's going to be married.

Sir HARRY.

To whom?

DUKE.

To *Kitty*.

Sir HARRY.

No!

DUKE.

Yes he is; and I intend to cuckold him.

Sir HARRY.

Then we may depend upon your Grace for cer-tain. Ha, ha, ha!

DUKE.

If our Houfe breaks up in a tolerable Time, I'll be with you.——Have you any Thing for us?

Sir

Sir H A R R Y.

Yes, a little Bit of Poetry——I muſt be at the *Cocoa-Tree* myſelf till eight.

D U K E.

Heigh ho!—I am quite out of Spirits—I had a damn'd Debauch laſt Night, Baronet.——Lord *Francis, Bob* the Biſhop, and I, tipt off four Bottles of *Burgundy* a-piece—Ha! there are two fine Girls coming! Faith—Lady *Bab*—aye, and Lady *Charlotte*—— 　　　　　　　　　　　[*Takes out his Glaſs.*

Sir H A R R Y.

We'll not join them.

D U K E.

..Oh, yes—*Bab* is a fine Wench, notwithſtanding her Complexion; tho' I ſhould be glad ſhe would keep her Teeth cleaner——Your *Engliſh* Women are damn'd negligent about their Teeth.——How is your *Charlotte* in that Particular?

Sir H A R R Y.

My *Charlotte!*

D U K E.

Aye, the World ſays, you are to have her.

Sir H A R R Y.

I own I did keep her Company; but we are off, my Lord.

D U K E.

How ſo?

Sir H A R R Y.

Between you and me ſhe has a plaguy thick Pair of Legs.

D U K E.

Oh, damn it—that's inſufferable.

Sir H A R R Y.

Beſides, ſhe's a Fool, and miſs'd her Opportunity with the old Counteſs.

D U K E.

I am afraid, Baronet, you love Money.——Rot it, I never ſave a Shilling—Indeed I am ſure of a
　　　　　　　　　　　　　　　　　　　Place

Place in the Excise—Lady *Charlotte* is to be of the Party To-night ; how do you manage that ?

Sir HARRY.

Why, we do meet at a third Place, are very civil, and look queer, and laugh, and abuse one another, and all that.

D K U E.

A-la-mode, ha!——Here they are.

Sir HARRY.

Let us retire.   [*They retire.*

Enter Lady BAB's *Maid, and Lady*
CHARLOTTE's *Maid.*

Lady BAB.

Oh! fie! Lady *Charlotte*, you are quite indelicate ! I am sorry for your Taste !

Lady CHARLOTTE.

Well, I say it again, I love *Vaux-hall.*

Lady BAB.

O my Stars! Why there is no body there but filthy Citizens.

Lady CHARLOTTE.

We were in Hopes the raising the Price would have kept them out, ha, ha, ha!

Lady BAB.

Ha, ha, ha!——*Runelow* for my Money.

Lady CHARLOTTE.

Now you talk of *Runelow*, when did you see the Colonel, Lady *Bab ?*

Lady BAB.

The Colonel! I hate the Fellow.—He had the Assurance to talk of a Creature in *Glocestershire* before may Face.

Lady CHARLOTTE.

He is a pretty Man for all that—Soldiers, you know, have their Mistresses every where.

Lady

Lady BAB.

I defpife him——How goes on your Affair with the Boronet?

Lady CHARLOTTE.

The Baronet is a ftupid Wretch, and I fhall have nothing to fay to him——You are to be at *Lovel*'s To-night, Lady *Bab*?

Lady BAB.

Unlefs I alter my Mind—I don't admire vifiting thefe Commoners, Lady *Charlotte*.

Lady CHARLOTTE.

Oh, but Mrs. *Kitty* has Tafte.

Lady BAB.

She affects it.

Lady CHARLOTTE.

The Duke is fond of her, and he has Judgment.

Lady BAB.

The Duke might fhew his Judgment much better.
                              [*Holding up her Head.*

Lady CHARLOTTE.

There he is, and the Baronet too —— Take no Notice of them——We'll rally them by-and-by.

Lady BAB.

Dull Souls! Let us fet up a loud Laugh, and leave 'em.

Lady CHARLOTTE.

Ay;—Let us be gone; for the common People do fo ftare at us—we fhall certainly be mobb'd.

BOTH.

Ha, ha, ha ——Ha, ha, ha!   [*Exeunt.*

DUKE and Sir HARRY come forward.

DUKE.

They certainly faw us, and are gone off laughing at us —— I muft follow ——

Sir HARRY.

No, no.

DUKE.

DUKE.

I muſt, —I muſt have a Party of Raillery with them, a bon mot or ſo. Sir *Harry*, you'll excuſe me.——Adieu, I'll be with you in the Evening, if poſſible; though, hark ye! there is a Bill depending in our Houſe, which the Miniſtry make a Point of our attending; and ſo you know, Mum! we muſt mind the Stops of the Great Fiddle.—Adieu. [*Ex.*

Sir HARRY.

What a Coxcomb this is! and the Fellow can't read. It was but the other Day that he was Cowboy in the Country, then was bound Prentice to a Perriwig-maker, got into my Lord Duke's Family, and now ſets up for a fine Gentleman. *O Tempora, O Mores!*

Re-enter DUKE'S *Servant.*

DUKE.

Sir *Harry*, prithee what are we to do at *Lovel*'s when we come there?

Sir · HARRY.

We ſhall have the Fiddles, I ſuppoſe.

DUKE.

The Fiddles! I have done with Dancing ever ſince the laſt Fit of the Gout. I'll tell you what, my dear Boy, I poſitively cannot be with them, unleſs we have a little ———[*Makes a Motion as if with the Dice-box.*

Sir HARRY.

Fie, my Lord Duke.

DUKE.

Look ye, Baronet, I inſiſt on it.—Who the Devil of any Faſhion can poſſibly ſpend an Evening without it? But I ſhall loſe the Girls.—How grave you look, ha, ha, ha!—Well, let there be Fiddles.

Sir HARRY.

But, my dear Lord, I ſhall be quite miſerable without you. ———

C   DUKE.

D U K E.

Well, I won't be particular, I'll do as the reft do.
—Tol, lol, lol. [*Exit, finging and dancing.*

Sir H A R R Y, *folus.*

He had the Affurance, laft Winter, to court a
Tradefman's Daughter in the City, with Two Thou-
fand Pounds to her Fortune, —— and got me to
write his Love-Letters. He pretended to be an
Enfign in a marching Regiment ; fo wheedled the
old Folks into Confent, and would have carried the
Girl off, but was unluckily prevented by the Wafh-
erwoman, who happened to be his firft Coufin.

(*Enter* PHILIP.)

—— Mr. *Philip*, your Servant.

P H I L I P.

*Y*ou are welcome to *England*, Sir *Harry*; I hope
you received the Card, and will do us the Honour
of your Company—— My Mafter is gone into
Devonfhire——We'll have a roaring Night.

Sir H A R R Y.

I'll certainly wait on you.

P H I L I P.

The Girls will be with us.

Sir H A R R Y.

Is this a Wedding-Supper, *Philip ?*

P H I L I P.

What do you mean, Sir *Harry ?*

Sir H A R R Y.

The Duke tells me fo.

P H I L I P.

The Duke's a Fool.

Sir H A R R Y.

Take care what you fay ; his Grace is a Bruifer.

P H I L I P.

I am a Pupil of the fame Academy, and not
afraid of him, I affure you : Sir *Harry*, we'll have
a noble Batch —— I have fuch Wine for you!

Sir

Sir HARRY.

I am your Man, *Phil.*

PHILIP.

Egad the Cellar fhall bleed: I have fome *Bur-gundy* that is fit for an Emperor —————— My Mafter would have given his Ears for fome of it t'other Day, to treat my Lord What d'ye-call-him with; but I told him it was all gone; ha! Charity begins at home, ha! —— Odfo, here is Mr. *Freeman*, my Mafter's intimate Friend; he's a dry one. ————— Don't let us be feen together — He'll fufpect fome-thing.

Sir HARRY.

I am gone.

PHILIP.

Away, away, —— Remember — *Burgundy* is the Word.

Sir HARRY.

Right — Long Corks! ha, *Phil!* [*Mimicks the drawing of a Cork.*]—Your's. [*Exit.*

PHILIP.

Now for a Caft of my Office——A ftarch Phiz, a canting Phrafe, and as many Lies as neceffary.—Hem!

Enter FREEMAN.

FREEMAN.

Oh! *Philip*—How do you do, *Philip?*—You have loft your Mafter, I find.

PHILIP.

It is a Lofs indeed, Sir.—So good a Gentleman! — He muft be nearly got into *Devonfhire* by this Time——Sir, your Servant. [*Going.*

FREEMAN.

Why in fuch a Hurry, *Philip?*

PHILIP.

I fhall leave the Houfe as little as poffible, now his Honour is away.

C 2 FREEMAN.

FREEMAN.

You are in the right, *Philip*.

PHILIP.

Servants at fuch Times are too apt to be negligent and extravagant, Sir.

FREEMAN.

True; the Mafter's Abfence is the Time to try a good Servant in.

PHILIP.

It is fo, Sir: Sir, your Servant.   [*Going*.

FREEMAN.

Oh! Mr. *Philip*—pray ftay—you muft do me a Piece of Service.

PHILIP.

You command me, Sir ——   [*Bows*.

FREEMAN.

I look upon you, *Philip*, as one of the beft be-haved, moft fenfible, compleateft [Philip *bows*] Rafcals in the World.   [*Afide*.

PHILIP.

Your Honour is pleafed to compliment.

FREEMAN.

There is a Tenant of mine in *Effex*, a very honeft Man——Poor Fellow, he has a great Number of Children; and they have fent me one of 'em; a tall, gawky Boy, to make a Servant of; but my Folks fay, they can do nothing with him.

PHILIP.

Let me have him, Sir.

FREEMAN.

In Truth, he is an unlick'd Cub.

PHILIP.

I will lick him into fomething, I warrant you, Sir. —— Now my Mafter is abfent, I fhall have a good deal of Time upon my Hands; and I hate to be idle, Sir; in two Months I'll engage to finifh him.

FREEMAN.

FREEMAN.

I don't doubt it.   [*Aside.*

PHILIP.

Sir, I have twenty Pupils in the Parifh of St. *James*'s ; and for a Table, or a Side-board, cr behind an Equipage, or in the Delivery of a Meffage, or any thing——

FREEMAN.

What have you for Entrance?

PHILIP.

I always leave it to Gentlemens Generofity.

FREEMAN.

Here is a Guinea—— I beg he may be taken Care of.

PHILIP.

That he fhall, I promife you [*Aside.*] Your Honour knows me.

FREEMAN.

Thoroughly.   [*Aside.*

PHILIP.

When can I fee him, Sir?

FREEMAN.

Now, directly—call at my Houfe, and take him in your Hand.

PHILIP.

Sir, I will be with you in a Minute —— I will but ftep into the Market, to let the Tradefmen know they muft not truft any of our Servants, now they are at Board-wages——Humph!

FREEMAN.

How happy is Mr. *Lovel* in fo excellent a Servant!   [*Exit.*

PHILIP.

Ha, ha, ha! This is one of my Mafter's prudent Friends, who dines with him three Times a-Week, and thinks he is mighty generous in giving me five Guineas at *Chriftmas* —— Damn all fuch fneaking Scoundrels, I fay.   [*Exit.*

SCENE

SCENE, *The Servant's Hall in* LOVEL'S *Houſe.*

KINGSTON *and* COACHMAN, *drunk and ſleepy.*
[*Knocking at the Door.*

KINGSTON.

Somebody knocks———Coachy, go———go to the Door, Coachy———

COACHMAN.

I'll not go———do you go———you black Dog.

KINGSTON.

Devil ſhall fetch me, if I go.   [*Knocking.*

COACHMAN.

Why then let 'em ſtay———I'll not go—Damme ——Aye, knock the Door down, and let yourſelf in.   [*Knocking.*

KINGSTON.

Ay, ay ; knock again—knock again ——

COACHMAN.

Maſter is gone into *Devonſhire* — So he can't be there—So I'll go to ſleep.——

KINGSTON.

So will I—I'll go to ſleep too.

COACHMAN.

You lye, Devil———you ſhall not go to ſleep till I am aſleep——I am King of the Kitchen.

KINGSTON.

No, you are not King ; but when you are drunk, you are ſulky as a Hell.—Here is Cooky coming —She is King and Queen too.

Enter COOK.

COOK.

Somebody has knock'd at the Door twenty Times, and nobody hears ——Why, Coachman— *Kingſton*———Ye drunken Bears, why don't one of you go to the Door ?

COACHMAN.

COACHMAN.

You go, Cook; you go——

COOK.

Hang me, if I go——

KINGSTON.

Yes, yes, Cooky go; *Mollſy, Pollſy* go.——

COOK.

Out you Black Toad———It is none of my
Buſineſs, and go I will not.   [*Sits down.*

Enter PHILIP, *with* LOVEL *diſguis'd.*

PHILIP.

I might have ſtaid at the Door all Night, as the
little Man in the Play ſays, if I had not had the
Key of the Door in my Pocket——What is come
to you all?

COOK.

There is *John* Coachman, and *Kingſton,* as drunk
as two Bears.

PHILIP.

Ah, ha! my Lads, what, finiſh'd already? Theſe
are the very beſt of Servants——Poor Fellows, I
ſuppoſe they have been drinking their Maſter's
good Journey——ha, ha, ha!

LOVEL.

No doubt on't.   [*Aſide.*

PHILIP.

Yo ho! get to Bed, you Dogs, and ſleep your-
ſelves ſober, that you may be able to get drunk
again by-and-by—They are as faſt as a Church—
Jemmy.

LOVEL.

Anon?

PHILIP.

Do you love Drinking?

LOVEL.

Yes,—I loves Ale.

PHILIP.

PHILIP.

—You Dog, you fhall fwim in *Burgundy*.

LOVEL.

Burgundy! what's that ?

PHILIP.

Cook, wake thofe honeft Gentlemen, and fend them to Bed.

COOK.

It is impoffible to wake them.

LOVEL.

I think I could wake 'em, Sir, if I might—Heh—

PHILIP.

Do *Jemmy*, wake 'em *Jemmy*—ha, ha, ha !

LOVEL.

Hip,—Mr. Coachman.   [*Gives him a great Slap on the Face.*

COACHMAN.

Oh! oh! What ? Zounds! Oh!—Damn you !—

LOVEL.

What, Blackey! Blackey! [*Pulls him by the Nofe.*

KINGSTON.

Oh! oh !——What now ! Curfe you ! Oh !—— Cot tam you.

LOVEL.

Ha, ha, ha !

PHILIP.

Ha, ha, ha !—Well done *Jemmy*. —— Cook, fee thofe Gentry to Bed.

COOK.

Marry come up, I fay fo too ; not I indeed.—

COACHMAN.

She fhan't fee us to Bed—We'll fee ourfelves to Bed.

KINGSTON.

We got drunk together, and we'll go to Bed together.   [*Exeunt, reeling.*

PHILIP.

PHILIP.

You fee how we live, Boy.

LOVEL.

Yes, I *fees* how you live.——

PHILIP.

Let the Supper be elegant, Cook.

COOK.

Who pays for it ?

PHILIP.

My Mafter to be fure : Who elfe ? ha, ha, ha!
He is rich enough, I hope, ha, ha, ha !

LOVEL.

Humh.   [*Afide.*

PHILIP.

Each of us muft take a Part, and fink it in our
next weekly Bills ; that is the way.

LOVEL.

Soh !   [*Afide.*

COOK.

Prithee *Philip*, what Boy is this ?

PHILIP.

A Boy of *Freeman*'s recommending.

LOVEL.

Yes, I'm 'Squire *Freeman*'s Boy,——Heh——

COOK.

Freeman is a ftingy Hound, and you may tell him
I fay fo.   He dines here three times a Week, and I
never faw the Colour of his Money yet.

LOVEL.

Ha, ha, ha, That is good————*Freeman* fhall
have it.   [*Afide.*

COOK.

I muft ftep to the Tallow-Chandler's, to difpofe
of fome of my Perquifites; and then I'll fet about
Supper.————

D

PHILIP.

PHILIP.

Well faid, Cook, that is right, the Perquifite is the Thing, Cook.

COOK.

Cloe, Cloe, where are you, *Cloe*—— [*Calls.*

Enter CLOE.

CLOE.

Yes, Miftrefs.——

COOK.

Take that box and follow me. [*Exit.*

CLOE.

Yes, Miftrefs; [*Takes the Box.*]——Who is this? [*feeing* Lovel.] Hee, hee, hee. —— Oh —— This is pretty Boy——Hee, hee, hee.——Oh——This is pretty Red Hair, hee, hee, hee——You fhall be in love with me by-and-by——Hee, hee. [*Exit.* *chucking* Lovel *under the Chin.*

LOVEL.

A very pretty Amour. [*Afide.*] Oh la! what a fine Room is this—Is this the Dining Room, pray Sir?

PHILIP.

No, our Drinking Room.

LOVEL.

La! la! What a fine Lady here is.—This is Madam, I fuppofe.

Enter KITTY.

PHILIP.

Where have you been *Kitty?*

KITTY.

I have been difpofing of fome of his Honour's Shirts, and other Linen, which it is a Shame his Honour fhould wear any longer.——Mother *Barter* is above, and waits to know if you have any Commands for her.

PHILIP.

I fhall difpofe of my Wardrobe to-morrow.

KITTY.

Who have we here? [Lovel *bows.*

PHILIP.

PHILIP.

A Boy of *Freeman*'s, a poor filly Fool——

LOVEL.

Thank you——   [*Afide.*

PHILIP.

I intend the Entertainment this Evening as a Compliment to you *Kitty.*

KITTY.

I am your humble, Mr. *Philip.*

PHILIP.

But I beg I may fee none of your Airs, or hear any of your *French* Gibberifh with the Duke.

KITTY.

Don't be jealous, *Phil.*   [*Fawningly.*

PHILIP.

I intend, before our Marriage, to fettle fome-thing handfome upon you, and with the five hundred Pounds which I have already faved in this extra-vagant Fellow's Family——

LOVEL.

A Dog! [*Afide*] —— O la, la, what, have you got five hundred Pounds ?

PHILIP.

Peace, Blockhead——

KITTY.

I'll tell you what you fhall do, *Phil.*

PHILIP.

Aye, what fhall I do ?

KITTY.

You fhall fet up a Chocolate-houfe, my Dear——

PHILIP.

Yes, and be cuckolded ——   [*Apart.*

KITTY.

You know my Education was a very genteel one—I was a Half-boarder at *Chelfea,* and I fpeak *French* like a Native—*Comment vcus porter vous, Mounfieur.*   [*Awkardly.*

PHILIP.

Pſha! Pſha!————

KITTY.

One is nothing without *French* — I ſhall ſhine in the Bar — Do you ſpeak *French*, Boy ?

LOVEL.

Anon————

KITTY.

Anon — O the Fool! ha, ha, ha !—Come here, do, and let me new mold you a little—you muſt be a good Boy, and wait upon the Gentlefolks To-night.　　　　　　　[*She ties and powders his Hair.*

LOVEL.

Yes, a'n't pleaſe you, I'll do my beſt.

KITTY.

His beſt! O the Natural!—This is a ſtrange Head of Hair of thine, Boy—It is ſo coarſe, and ſo carotty.

LOVEL.

All my Brothers and Siſters be red in the Pole.

PHILIP—KITTY.

Ha, ha, ha !————　　　　　　[*Loud Laugh.*

KITTY.

There—Now you are ſomething like——Come, *Philip*, give the Boy a Leſſon, and then I'll lecture him out of the *Servant's Guide.*

PHILIP.

Come, Sir, firſt, Hold up your Head — very well—Turn out your Toes, Sir,—very well—Now call Coach——

LOVEL.

What is call Coach ?

PHILIP.

Thus, Sir: Coach, Coach, Coach.　　　　[*Loud.*

LOVEL.

Coach, Coach, Coach.　　　　／　　[*Imitating.*

PHILIP.

PHILIP.

Admirable! the Knave has a good Ear—Now, Sir, tell me a Lye.

LOVEL.

O la! I never told a Lye in all my Life.

PHILIP.

Then it is high Time you fhould begin now; what is a Servant good for that can't tell a Lye?

KITTY.

And ftand in it—Now I'll lecture him [*Takes out a Book*] This is *The Servant's Guide to Wealth, by* Timothy Shoulderknot, *formerly Servant to feveral Noblemen, and now an Officer in the Cuftoms; Neceffary for all Servants.*

PHILIP.

Mind, Sir, what excellent Rules the Book contains, and remember them well——Come, *Kitty*, begin——

KITTY *(Reads.)*

Advice to the Footman.

" Let it for ever be your plan
" To be the Mafter, not the Man,
" And do as little as you can.

LOVEL.

He, he, he!——Yes, I'll do nothing at all—— not I.

KITTY.

" At Market never think it Stealing,
" To keep with Tradefmen *proper* Dealing;
" All Stewards have a fellow-feeling.

PHILIP.

You will underftand that better one Day or other, Boy.

KITTY.

To the Groom.

" Never allow your Mafter able
" To judge of Matters in the Stable:

" If

" If he fhould roughly fpeak his Mind,
" Or to difmifs you feems inclin'd,
" Lame the beft Horfe, or break his Wind.

LOVEL.

Oddines! that's good — he, he, he!

KITTY.

To the Coachman.

" If your good Mafter on you doats,
    " Ne'er leave his Houfe to ferve a Stranger,
" But pocket Hay, and Straw, and Oats,
    " And let the Horfes eat the Manger.

LOVEL.

Eat the Manger! he, he, he!

KITTY.

I won't give you too much at a Time—Here Boy, take the Book, and read it every Night and Morning before you fay your Prayers.

PHILIP.

Ha, ha, ha!—very good, but now for Bufinefs.

KITTY.

Right——I'll go and get one of the Damafk Table-cloaths, and fome Napkins; and be fure, *Phil.* your Side-board is very fmart.   [*Exit.*

PHILIP.

That it fhall——Come, *Jemmy*——   [*Exit.*

LOVEL.

Soh!——Soh!——It works well.   [*Exit.*

END of the FIRST ACT.

ACT

ACT II.

SCENE, *The Servants Hall, with the Supper and Side-Board set out.*

PHILIP, KITTY, *and* LOVEL.

KITTY.

WELL, *Phil.* what think you? Don't we look very smart?——Now let 'em come as soon as they will, we shall be ready for 'em.

PHILIP.

'Tis all very well; but ———

KITTY.

But what?

PHILIP.

Why, I wish we could get that snarling Cur, *Tom*, to make one.

KITTY.

What is the matter with him?

PHILIP.

I don't know——he is a queer Son of a——

KITTY.

Oh, I know him; he is one of your sneaking half-bred Fellows, that prefers his Master's Interest to his own.

PHILIP.

——Here he is.

(*Enter* TOM.)

——And why won't you make one To-night, *Tom?*—— Here's Cook and Coachman, and all of us.

TOM.

T O M.

I tell you again I will not make one.

P H I L I P.

We fhall have fomething that's good.

T O M.

And make your Mafter pay for it.

P H I L I P.

I warrant, now, you think yourfelf mighty honeft——Ha, ha, ha!

T O M.

A little honefter than you, I hope, and not brag
neither.

K I T T Y.

Hark'e you, Mr. Honefty, don't be faucy——

L O V E L.

This is worth liftening to.   [*Afide.*

T O M.

What, Madam, you are afraid for your Cully,
are you?

K I T T Y.

Cully, Sirrah, Cully! Afraid, Sirrah! afraid of
what?   [*Goes up to* Tom.

P H I L I P.

Aye, Sir, afraid of what? [*Goes up on the other Side.*

L O V E L.

Aye, Sir, afraid of what?   [*Goes up too.*

T O M.

I value none of you—I know your Tricks.

P H I L I P.

What do you know, Sirrah?

K I T T Y.

Ay, what do you know?

L O V E L.

Ay, Sir, what do you know?

TOM.

TOM.

I know that you Two are in Fee with every Tradefman belonging to the Houfe —— And that you, Mr. *Clodpole*, are in a fair Way to be hang'd.

[*Strikes* Lovel.

PHILIP.

What do you ftrike the Boy for ?

LOVEL.

It is an honeft Blow.   [*Afide.*

TOM.

I'll ftrike him again.——'Tis fuch as you that bring a Scandal upon us all.

KITTY.

Come, none of your Impudence, *Tom.*

TOM.

Egad, Madam, the Gentry may well complain, when they get fuch Servants as you in their Houfes. —There's your good Friend, Mother *Barter*, the Old-Cloaths Woman, the greateft Thief in Town, juft now gone out with her Apron full of his Honour's Linen.

KITTY.

Well, Sir ; and did you never——ha ?

TOM.

No, never : I have lived with his Honour four Years, and never took the Value of that [*Snapping his Fingers.*]—His Honour is a Prince, gives noble Wages, and keeps noble Company, and yet you two are not contented, but cheat him wherever you can lay your Fingers.—Shame on you !——

LOVEL.

The Fellow I thought a Rogue, is the only honeft Servant in my Houfe.   [*Afide.*

KITTY.

Out you mealy-mouth'd Cur !

PHILIP.

Well, go tell his Honour, do——ha, ha, ha !

E   TOM.

T O M.

I ſcorn that—Damn an Informer ! —— but yet,
I hope his Honour will find you two out, one Day
or other——That's all.——　　　　　　　[*Exit.*

K I T T Y.

This Fellow muſt be taken Care of.

P H I L I P.

I'll do his Buſineſs for him, when his Honour
comes to Town.

L O V E L.

You lye, you Scoundrel ; you will not. 　[*Aſide·*
——O la ! here is a fine Gentleman.

Enter DUKE's *Servant.*

D U K E.

Ah ! ma chere Mademſeille ! Comment vous
portez vous ?　　　　　　　　　　　[*Salute.*

K I T T Y.

Fort bien, je vous remercier, Monſieur.

P H I L I P.

Now we ſhall have Nonſenſe by Wholeſale.

D U K E.

How do you do, *Philip?*

P H I L I P.

Your Grace's humble Servant.

D U K E.

But my dear *Kitty*——　　　　　　　[*Talk apart.*

P H I L I P.

Jemmy.

L O V E L.

Anon ?

P H I L I P.

Come along with me, and I will make you free
of the Cellar.

L O V E L.

Yes—I will—But won't you aſk *he* to drink ?

P H I L I P.

No, no ; he will have his Share by-and-by.—
Come along.

L O V E L.

L O V E L.

Yes.   [*Exeunt* Philip *and* Lovel.

K I T T Y.

Indeed I thought your Grace an Age in coming.

D U K E.

Upon Honour, our Houfe is but this Moment up.—You have a damn'd vile Collection of Pictures I obferve, above Stairs, *Kitty*——Your 'Squire has no Tafte.——

K I T T Y.

No Tafte! That's impoffible, for he has laid out a vaft deal of Money.

D U K E.

There is not an original Picture in the whole Collection——Where could he pick 'em up?

K I T T Y.

He employs three or four Men to buy for him, and he always pays for Originals.

D U K E.

Donnez moi votre Eau de Luce——My Head aches confoundedly [*She gives a Smelling-Bottle*]—*Kitty*, my dear, I hear you are going to be married.—

K I T T Y.

Pardonnez moi, for that.

D U K E.

If you get a Boy, I'll be Godfather, Faith.—

K I T T Y.

How you rattle, Duke!———— I am thinking, my Lord, when I had the Honour to fee you laft.

D U K E.

At the Play, Mademfeille.——

K I T T Y.

Your Grace loves a Play?

E 2   DUKE.

D U K E.

No——It is a dull, old-fafhioned Entertainment
—I hate it.——

K I T T Y.

Well, give me a good Tragedy.

D U K E.

It muſt not be a modern one then—You are deviliſh handſome, *Kate*—Kiſs me—[*Offers to kiſs her.*

(Enter Sir HARRY's *Servant.)*

Sir H A R R Y.

Oh oh!—Are you thereabouts, my Lord Duke?
That may do very well by-and-by——However,
you'll never find me behind-hand.　　　[*Offers to
kiſs her.*

D U K E.

Stand off, you are a Commoner—Nothing under
Nobility approaches *Kitty.*

Sir H A R R Y.

You are ſo deviliſh proud of your Nobility——
Now, I think, we have more true Nobility than
you —— Let me tell you, Sir, a Knight of the
Shire ——

D U K E.

A Knight of the Shire! ha, ha, ha! a mighty
Honour, truly, to repreſent all the Fools in the
County.

K I T T Y.

O Lud! this is charming to ſee two Noblemen
quarrel.

Sir H A R R Y.

Why, any Fool may be born to a Title, but only
a wiſe Man can make himſelf honourable.

K I T T Y.

Well ſaid, Sir *Harry*; that is good *Merillity.*

DUKE.

D.U K E.

I hope you make fome Difference between Hereditary Honours and the Huzzas of a Mob.

K I T T Y.

Very fmart, my Lord—Now, Sir *Harry*——

Sir H A R R Y.

If you make ufe of your Hereditary Honours to fcreen you from Debt——

D U K E.

Zounds! Sir, what do you mean by that?

K I T T Y.

Hold, hold! I fhall have fome fine old Noble Blood fpilt here——Ha' done, Sir *Harry*——

Sir H A R R Y.

Not I—Why he is always valuing himfelf upon his upper Houfe.

D U K E.

We have Dignity.   [*Slow,*

Sir H A R R Y.

But what becomes of your Dignity, if we refufe the Supplies?   [*Quick.*

K I T T Y.

Peace, Peace——Here's Lady *Bab*——

(*Enter Lady* B A B*'s Servant in a Chair.*)

Dear Lady *Bab*————

Lady B A B.

Mrs. *Kitty*, your Servant—I was afraid of taking Cold, and fo ordered the Chair down Stairs. Well, and how do you do? —— My Lord Duke, your Servant——and Sir *Harry* too——your's.

D U K E.

Your Ladyfhip's devoted——

Lady B A B.

I'm afraid I have trefpaffed in Point of Time ——[*Looks on her Watch.* —— But I got into my fav'rite Author.

DUKE.

D U K E.

Yes, I found her Ladyſhip at her Studies this
Morning——Some wicked Poem——

Lady B A B.

Oh you Wretch!—I never read but one Book.

K I T T Y.

What is your Ladyſhip ſo fond of?

Lady B A B.

Shikſpur. Did you never read *Shikſpur?*

K I T T Y. */ Ben Johnson*

Shikſpur! Shikſpur!—Who wrote it?——No, I
never read *Shikſpur.*   ^

Lady B A B.

Then you have an immenſe Pleaſure to come.

K I T T Y.

Well then, I'll read it over one Afternoon or
other.——Here's Lady *Charlotte.*——

(Enter Lady CHARLOTTE's *Maid in a Chair.)*
—Dear Lady *Charlotte.*

Lady C H A R L O T T E.

Oh, Mrs. *Kitty,* I thought I never ſhould have
reach'd your Houſe —— Such a Fit of the Cholic
ſeiz'd me —— Oh, Lady *Bab,* how long has your
Ladyſhip been here?——My Chairmen were ſuch
Drones——My Lord Duke! the Pink of all good
Breeding.

D U K E.

Oh Ma'm——   [*Bowing.*

Lady C H A R L O T T E.

And Sir *Harry* —— Your Servant, Sir *Harry.*
                   [*Formally.*

Sir H A R R Y.

Madam, your Servant — I am ſorry to hear your
Ladyſhip has been ill.——

Lady C H A R L O T T E.

You muſt give me Leave to doubt the Sincerity
of that Sorrow, Sir ——Remember the *Park.*——

Sir

Sir HARRY.

The *Park!* I'll explain that Affair, Madam.

Lady CHARLOTTE.

I want none of your Explanations.   [*Scornfully.*

Sir HARRY.

Dear Lady *Charlotte!*

Lady CHARLOTTE.

No, Sir; I have obferv'd your Coolnefs of late, and defpife you——A trumpery Baronet!

Sir HARRY.

I fee how it is; nothing will fatisfy you but Nobility——That fly Dog the Marquis——

Lady CHARLOTTE.

None of your Reflections, Sir——The Marquis is a Perfon of Honour, and above enquiring after a Lady's Fortune, as you meanly did.

Sir HARRY.

I—I—Madam? —I fcorn fuch a Thing —— I affure you, Madam, I never—That is to fay—— Egad I am confounded——My Lord Duke, what fhall I fay to her?—Pray help me out.—   [*Afide.*

DUKE.

Afk her to fhew her Legs—Ha, ha, ha! [*Afide.*

Enter PHILIP *and* LOVEL, *loaded with Bottles.*

PHILIP.

Here my little Peer —— Here is Wine that will ennoble your Blood——Both your Ladyfhips moft humble Servant.

LOVEL. [*Affecting to be drunk.*]

Both your Ladyfhips moft humble Servant.

KITTY.

Why, *Philip,* you have made the Boy drunk.

PHILIP.

I have made him free of the Cellar. Ha, ha, ha!

LOVEL.

L O V E L.

Yes, I am free—I am very free.———

P H I L I P.

He has had a Smack of every Sort of Wine, from humble Port to Imperial Tokay.

L O V E L.

Yes, I have been drinking *Kokay.*

K I T T Y.

Go, get you fome Sleep, Child, that you may wait on his Lordfhip by-and-by.

L O V E L.

Thank you, Madam —— I will certainly wait on their Lordfhips, and their Ladyfhips too.   [*Afide, and exit.*

P H I L I P.

Well, Ladies, what fay you to a Dance, and then to Supper ? Have you had your Tea ?

A L L.

A Dance, a Dance—No Tea—No Tea.

P H I L I P.

Here, Fidler [*calls.*] I have provided a very good Hand, you fee.

(*Enter* FIDLER, *with a wooden Leg.*)

Sir H A R R Y.

Not fo well legg'd, Mr. *Philip.*

A L L.

Ha, ha, ha !

D U K E.

Le drole !—Harkye, Mr.—which Leg do you beat Time with ?

A L L.

Ha, ha, ha !   [*Loud Laugh.*

Sir H A R R Y.

What can you play, Domine ?

F I D L E R.

Any thing, an't pleafe your Honour, from a Jig to a Sonata.

P H I L I P.

PHILIP.

Come here —— Where are all our People ?
[*Enter* Coachman, Cook, Kingston, Cloe.] I'll
couple you — My Lord Duke will take *Kitty*, —
Lady *Bab* will do me the Honour of her Hand;
Sir *Harry* and Lady *Charlotte*——Coachman and
Cook, and the two Devils dance together ——
Ha, ha, ha!

DUKE.

With Submission, the Country Dances by-
and-by.

Lady CHARLOTTE.

Ay, ay; *French* Dances before Supper, and
Country Dances after—I beg the Duke and Mrs.
Kitty may give us a Minuet.

DUKE.

Dear Lady *Charlotte*, confider my poor Gout—
Sir *Harry* will oblige us.　　　[*Sir* Harry *bows*.

ALL.

—Minuet, Sir *Harry*—Minuet, Sir *Harry*——

FIDLER.

What Minuet would your Honours pleafe to
have ?

KITTY.

What Minuet?——Let me fee——Play *Marſhal*
Thingumbob's Minuet.

　　　[*A Minuet by Sir* Harry *and* Kitty, *awkard
　　　and conceited.*

Lady CHARLOTTE.

Mrs. *Kitty* dances fweetly.

PHILIP.

And Sir *Harry* delightfully.

DUKE.

Well enough for a Commoner.

PHILIP.

Come now to Supper —— A Gentleman and a
Lady—Here, Fidler [*gives Money*.] Wait without.
　　　F　　　　　FIDLER.

FIDLER.

Yes, an't pleafe your Honour.   [*Exit with a*
                                Tankard.

[*They fit down.*]

PHILIP.

We will fet the Wine on the Table — Here is
Claret, Burgundy, and Champagne, and a Bottle
of Tokay for the Ladies———There are Tickets on
every Bottle—If any Gentleman chufes Port—

DUKE.

Port !—'Tis only fit for a Dram.

KITTY.

Lady *Bab*, what fhall I fend you ?———Lady
Charlotte, pray be free ; the more free, the more
welcome, as they fay in my Country.———The
Gentlemen will be fo good as to take Care of them-
felves.   [*A Paufe.*

DUKE.

Lady *Charlotte*, " Hob or Nob !"

Lady CHARLOTTE.

Done —my Lord—in Burgundy, if you pleafe.

DUKE.

Here's your Sweetheart and mine, and the Friends
of the Company.   [*They drink. A Paufe.*

PHILIP.

Come Ladies and Gentlemen, a Bumper all
round—I have a Health for you—" Here is to the
" Amendment of our Mafters and Miftreffes."

ALL.

Ha, ha, ha, ha, ha, ha !   [*Loud Laugh. A*
                                  Paufe.

KITTY.

Ladies, pray what is your Opinion of a fingle
Gentleman's Service ?

Lady CHARLOTTE.

Do you mean an *old* fingle Gentleman ?

ALL.

Ha, ha, ha, ha, ha, ha !   [*Loud Laugh.*
                                  PHILIP.

PHILIP.

My Lord Duke, your Toaſt.

DUKE.

Lady *Betty*——

PHILIP.

Oh no—A Health and a Sentiment.

DUKE.

A Health and a Sentiment?——No, no, let us have a Song——Sir *Harry*, your Song.——

Sir HARRY.

Would you have it?——Well then—Mrs. *Kitty* we muſt call upon you —— Will you honour my Muſe?——

ALL.

A Song, a Song, ay, ay, Sir *Harry*'s Song—— Sir *Harry*'s Song—

DUKE.

A Song to be ſure, — but firſt,—Preludo——— [*Kiſſes* Kitty.]——Pray Gentlemen put it about.

[*Kiſſing round*——Kingſton *kiſſes* Cloe *heartily*.

Sir. HARRY.

See how the Devils kiſs!

KITTY.

I am really hoarſe; but—Hem—I muſt clear up my Pipes——Hem——This is Sir *Harry*'s Song; being a new Song, entitled and called,

The Fellow Servant, or All in a Livery.

[KITTY *Sings.*]

I.

Come here Fellow Servant, and liſten to me,
I'll ſhew you how thoſe of ſuperior Degree
Are only Dependants, no better than we.
    Chorus, *Both high and low in this do agree.*
        'Tis here Fellow Servant,
        And there Fellow Servant,
        And all in a Livery.

F 2

11

II.

See yonder fine Spark in Embroidery dreft,
Who bows to the Great, and if they fmile, is bleft ;
What is he? I'faith, but a Servant at beft.
   Cho. *Both high, &c.*

III.

Nature made all alike, no Diftinction fhe craves,
So we laugh at the great World, its Fools and its
   Knaves,
For we are all Servants, but they are all Slaves.
   ` `Cho. *Both high, &c.*

IV.

The fat fhining Glutton looks up to the Shelf,
The wrinkled lean Mifer bows down to his Pelf,
And the curl-pated Beau is a Slave to himfelf.
   Cho. *Both high, &c.*

V.

The gay fparkling Belle, who the whole Town alarms,
And with Eyes, Lips, and Neck, fets the Smarts all
   in Arms,
Is a Vaffal herfelf, a mere Drudge to her Charms.
   Cho. *Both high, &c.*

VI.

Then we'll drink like our Betters, and laugh, fing
   and love,
And when fick of one Place, to another we'll move,
For with Little and Great, the beft Joy is to rove.
  Chorus. *Both high and low in this do agree* .
   ` `*That 'tis here Fellow Servant,*
    And there Fellow Servant,
    And all in a Livery.

P H I L I P.

How do you like it my Lord Duke?

D U K E.

It is a damn'd vile compofition——

    P H I L I P. ` `

How fo?

          DUKE.

DUKE.

O very low! Very low indeed!

Sir HARRY.

Can you make a better?

DUKE.

I hope fo.

Sir HARRY.

That is very conceited.

DUKE.

What is conceited, you Scoundrel?

Sir HARRY.

Scoundrel! You are a Rafcal——I'll pull you by the Nofe——   [*All rife.*

DUKE.

Look ye, Friend; don't give yourfelf Airs, and make a Difturbance among the Ladies —— If you are a Gentleman, name your Weapons.

Sir HARRY.

Weapons! What you will—Piftols——

DUKE.

Done ——behind *Montague Houfe.*

Sir HARRY.

Done——with Seconds.

DUKE.

Done.——

PHILIP.

Oh for Shame, Gentlemen——My Lord Duke! ——Sir *Harry,* the Ladies! fie!   [*Duke and Sir Harry affect to fing.*

A violent Knocking.

PHILIP.

What the Devil can that be, *Kitty?*

KITTY.

Who can it poffibly be?

PHILIP.

Kingfton, run up Stairs and peep. [*Exit* Kingfton. It founds like my Mafter's Rap —— Pray Heaven

it

it is not he ;—— [*Enter* Kingfton] Well, *Kingfton*, what is it ?

KINGSTON.

It is Mafter and Mr. *Freeman*—— I peep'd thro' the Key-Hole, and faw them by the Lamp Light— *Tom* has juft let them in——

P H I L I P.

The Devil he has ! What can have brought him back ?

K I T T Y.

No Matter what——Away with the Things.—

P H I L I P.

Away with the Wine — Away with the Plate— Here Coachman, Cook, *Cloe*, *Kingfton* bear a Hand—Out with the Candles— Away, away.

[*They carry away the Table*, &c.

V I S I T E R S.

What fhall we do ? What fhall we do ?

[*They all run about in Confufion.*

K I T T Y.

Run up Stairs, Ladies.

P H I L I P.

No, no, no.——He'll fee you then——

Sir H A R R Y.

What the Devil had I to do here !

D U K E.

Pox take it, face it out.

Sir H A R R Y. ,

Oh no ; thefe *Weft-Indians* are very fiery.

P H I L I P.

I would not have him fee any of you for the World.

L O V E L *without.*

Philip——Where's *Philip ?*

P H I L I P.

Oh the Devil ! he's certainly coming down Stairs ——Sir *Harry*, run down into the Cellar —— My Lord Duke get into the Pantry——Away, away.

K I T T Y.

KITTY.

No, no; do you put their Ladyſhips into the Pantry, and I'll take his Grace into the Coal-hole.

VISITERS.

Any where, any. where —— Up the Chimney if you will.

PHILIP.

There——in with you.

[*They all go into the Pantry.*

LOVEL *without.*

Philip——*Philip.*————

PHILIP.

Coming, Sir—[*Aloud.*]—*Kitty*, have you never a good Book to be reading of?

KITTY.

Yes, here is *one.*

PHILIP.

'Egad, this is Black *Monday* with us—Sit down ——Seem to read your Book —— Here he is, as drunk as a Piper——. [*They ſit down.*

Enter LOVEL *with Piſtols, affecting to be drunk,* FREEMAN *following.*

LOVEL.

Philip, the Son of *Alexander* the Great, where are all my Myrmidons?——What the Devil makes you up ſo early this Morning?

PHILIP.

He is very drunk indeed—[*Aſide.*]—Mrs. *Kitty* and I had got into a good Book, your Honour.

FREEMAN.

Ay, ay, they have been well employed, I dare, ſay—ha, ha, ha!

LOVEL.

Come, ſit down, *Freeman*,—Lie you there. [*Lays his Piſtols down.*] I come a little unexpectedly, perhaps, *Philip.*

PHILIP.

PHILIP

A good Servant is never afraid of being caught, Sir————

L O V E L.

I have some Accounts that I muft fettle————

P H I L I P.

Accounts, Sir! To-night?

L O V E L.

Yes, To-night — I find myfelf perfectly clear — you fhall fee I'll fettle them in a Twinkling.

P H I L I P.

Your Honour will go into the Parlour?

L O V E L.

No, I'll fettle 'em all here.————

K I T T Y.

Your Honour muft not fit here.————

L O V E L.

Why not?

K I T T Y.

You will certainly take Cold, Sir, the Room has not been wafhed above an Hour.

L O V E L.

What a curfed Lye that is!   [*Afide*.

D U K E.

Philip.————*Philip.*————*Philip.*   [*Peeping out*.

P H I L I P.

Pox take you!————Hold your Tongue.— [*Afide*.

F R E E M A N.

You have juft nick'd them in the very Minute.
                                        [*Afide to* Lovel.

L O V E L.

I find I have————Mum————[*Afide to* Freeman.]
Get fome Wine, *Philip*————[*Exit* Philip.]————Tho'
I muft eat fomething before I drink————*Kitty*, what
have you got in the Pantry?

KITTY.

KITTY.

In the Pantry? Lard, your Honour! We are at Board-wages.——

FREEMAN.

I could eat a Morfel of cold Meat.

LOVEL.

You fhall have it——Here—[*Rifes.*]——Open the Pantry-door—I'll be about your Board-wages!—— I have treated you often, now you fhall treat your Mafter.——

KITTY.

If I may be believed, Sir, there is not a Scrap of any Thing in the World in the Pantry.

[*Oppofing him.*

LOVEL.

Well, then we muft be contented, *Freeman.* —Let us have a Cruft of Bread and a Bottle of Wine.

[*Sits down again.*

KITTY.

Sir, had not my Mafter better go to Bed?——

[*Makes Signs to* Freeman *that* Lovel *is drunk.*

LOVEL.

Bed! Not I —— I'll fit here all Night ——'Tis very pleafant; and nothing like Variety in Life.

Sir HARRY *(Peeping.)*

Mrs. *Kitty*, Mrs. *Kitty*——

KITTY.

Peace, on your Life.　　　　　　　　　　[*Afide.*

LOVEL.

Kitty, what Voice is that?

KITTY.

No-body's, Sir.——Hem——

(PHILIP *brings Wine.*)

LOVEL.

Soh——Very well——Now do you two march off——March off, I fay.————

G　　　　　　　　PHILIP.

PHILIP.

We can't think of leaving your Honour — For
Egad, if we do, we are undone.   [*Afide.*

LOVEL.

Begone——My Service to you, *Freeman*, —This
is good Stuff.——

FREEMAN.

Excellent.   [*Somebody in the Pantry fneezes.*

KITTY.

We are undone ; undone.   [*Afide.*

PHILIP.

Oh ! That is the Duke's damn'd Rapee.   [*Afide.*

LOVEL.

Didn't you hear a Noife, *Charles ?*

FREEMAN.

Somebody fneez'd, I thought.

LOVEL.

Damn it ! There are Thieves in the Houfe——
I'll be among 'em——   [*Takes a Piftol.*

KITTY.

Lack-a day, Sir, it was only the Cat——They
fometimes fneeze for all the World like a Chriftian
——Here, *Jack, Jack*——He has got a Cold, Sir,
——Pufs,——Pufs.——

LOVEL.

A Cold ? then I'll cure him ——— Here *Jack,
Jack,*——Pufs, Pufs.——

KITTY.

Your Honour won't be fo rafh———Pray your
Honour, don't. ——   [*Oppofing.*

LOVEL.

Stand off——Here *Freeman*—Here's a Barrel for
Bufinefs, with a Brace of Slugs, and well prim'd,
as you fee——*Freeman*—I'll hold you five to four
——Nay, I'll hold you two to one, I hit the Cat
thro' the Key-hole of that Pantry-door.

FREEMAN.

FREEMAN.

Try, try, but I think it impoſſible———

LOVEL.

I am a damn'd good Markſman. [*Cocks the Piſtol, and points it at the Pantry Door.*]———Now for it! [*A violent Shriek, and all is diſcovered.*]———Who the Devil are all theſe ? One,———two,———three,——— four——— *Pray Mr Philip whose are these* PHILIP.

PHILIP.

They are particular Friends of mine, Sir ; Servants to ſome Noblemen in the Neighbourhood.

LOVEL.

I told you there were Thieves in the Houſe.

FREEMAN.

Ha, ha, ha!

PHILIP.

I aſſure your Honour they have been entertained at our own Expence, upon my Word.

KITTY.

Yes, indeed, your Honour, if it was the laſt Word I had to ſpeak.———

LOVEL.

Take up that Bottle———[Philip *takes up a Bottle with a Ticket to it, and is going off.*] ——— Bring it back ——— do you uſually entertain your Company with *Tokay,* Monſieur ?

PHILIP.

I, Sir, treat with Wine!

LOVEL.

O yes, *from humble Port to imperial Tokay too. Yes, I loves Kokay.* [Mimicking himſelf.

PHILIP.

How !—*Jemmy,* my Maſter !

KITTY.

Jemmy! the Devil !———

PHILIP.

P H I L I P.

Your Honour is at prefent in liquor—But in the Morning, when your Honour is recovered, I will fet all to rights again.——

L O V E L, *(Changing his Countenance, and turning his Wig.)*

We'll fet all to rights now—There, I am fober, at your Service ——What have you to fay *Philip ?* [*Philip ftarts.*] You may well ftart —— Go, get out of my Sight.

D U K E.

Sir—I have not the Honour to be known to you, but I have the Honour to ferve his Grace the Duke of————

L O V E L.

And the Impudence familiarly to affume his Title—Your Grace will give me leave to tell you, " That is the Door" —— And if you ever enter there again, I affure you, my Lord Duke, I will break every Bone in your Grace's Skin——Begone ——I beg their Ladyfhip's pardon, perhaps they cannot go without Chairs—Ha, ha, ha!

F R E E M A N.

Ha, ha, ha!   [*Sir* Harry *fteals off.*

D U K E.

Low-bred Fellows!   [*Exit.*

Lady C H A R L O T T E.

I thought how this Vifit would turn out.   [*Exit.*

Lady B A B.

They are downright *Hottenpots.*   [*Exit.*

P H I L I P and K I T T Y.

I hope your Honour will not take away our Bread.

L O V E L.

LOVEL.

" Five Hundred Pounds will fet you up in a
" Chocolate Houfe —— You'll fhine in the Bar,
" Madam " — I have been an Eye-witnefs of your
Roguery, Extravagance, and Ingratitude.

PHILIP and KITTY.

Oh, Sir —— Good Sir !

LOVEL.

You, Madam, may ftay here till To-morrow
Morning——And there, Madam, is the Book you
lent me, which I beg you'll read " Night and
" Morning before you fay your Prayers."

KITTY.

I am ruin'd and undone.——   [Exit.

LOVEL.

But you, Sir, for your Villainy, and (what I
hate worfe) your Hypocrify, fhall not ftay a Minute longer in this Houfe ; and here comes an
honeft Man to fhew you the Way out—Your Keys,
Sir.——   [Philip gives the Keys.

Enter TOM.

Tom, I refpeft and value you—You are an honeft Servant, and fhall never want Encouragement
—Be fo good, *Tom*, as to fee that Gentleman out
of my Houfe'[Points to Philip]——and then take
Charge of the Cellar and Plate.

TOM.

I thank your Honour ; but I would not rife on
the Ruin of a Fellow-fervant.

LOVEL.

No Remonftrances, *Tom*; it fhall be as I fay.—

PHILIP.

What a curfed Fool have I been ?
          [*Exeunt Servants.*

LOVEL.

L O V E L.

Well, *Charles*, I muſt thank you for my Frolick
——It has been a wholſome one to me———Have I
done right ?

F R E E M A N.

Entirely —— No Judge could have determin'd
better———As you puniſh'd the Bad, it was but
Juſtice to reward the Good.———

L O V E L.

A faithful Servant is a worthy Character.

F R E E M A N.

And can never receive too much Encouragement.

L O V E L.

Right.

F R E E M A N.

You have made *Tom* very happy.

L O V E L.

And I intend to make your *Robert* ſo too———
Every honeſt Servant ſhould be made happy.

F R E E M A N.

But what an inſufferable Piece of Aſſurance is it
in ſome of theſe Fellows to affect and imitate their
Maſter's Manners ?

L O V E L.

What Manners muſt thoſe be, which they can
imitate ?

F R E E M A N.

True.

L O V E L.

If Perſons of Rank would act up to their
Standard, it would be impoſſible that their Servants
could ape them—But when they affect every Thing
that is ridiculous, it will be in the Power of any low
Creature to follow their Example.

T H E   E N D.

Advertisement.

THE Author of this Piece, who is neither Mr. *Garrick* nor Mr. *Newbery*, begs Leave to obferve, that the large Body of Men, who have been offended at the Performance, are by no means the principal Perfons cenfured in it. They are made the Inftruments of conveying the Satire, and therefore it is not unnatural for them to miftake the Object of it. Proper Juftice has been done to their real Merit, by the fame Author, in an Apology for them, publifhed in a Six-penny Pamphlet, printed for Mr. *Newbery*, under the Name of *Oliver Grey*; where their Caufe is vindicated, and the Character of thofe Perfons fet forth, who, tho' placed in a fuperior Station of Life, by acting improperly in it, afford much jufter Matter for Cenfure and Ridicule.

www.ingramcontent.com/pod-product-compliance
Lightning Source LLC
Chambersburg PA
CBHW031930060726

47496CB00008BA/2789